STORY BY
GINGER GRABERT SPEDALE

ILLUSTRATED BY
MIKE S. HENRY

One sunny, humid day, deep in Louisiana, a little girl named Ruby Rose spied something spectacular!

From the familiar position of her old car seat, Ruby Rose stared in awe at the colors and shapes that dangled from the branches passing by.

"Mommy, Mommy... LOOOOOOK!
They are so pretty!" exclaimed Ruby Rose.

Confused, Mom said,
"What do you see, Ruby Rose?
I don't see anything."

Ruby Rose was sad
as the bright colors
swiftly passed her by.
But, shortly after, she
spotted them again.

"Mommy, look!
I see them again.
Beads!
Beads on trees!"

"Can we go to a parade tonight? Pleeeeez?" begged Ruby Rose

"Not tonight, Ruby Rose. There are no parades until next year," explained Mom.

"But why don't you tell me what you like best about Mardi Gras time?"

Ruby Rose began to list
her favorite moments.

"I like when
everyone gets
dressed up in
costumes."

"I like when we see the Mardi Gras Indians and hear the music of the marching bands."

"I like when we eat cold fried chicken and King Cake all day!"

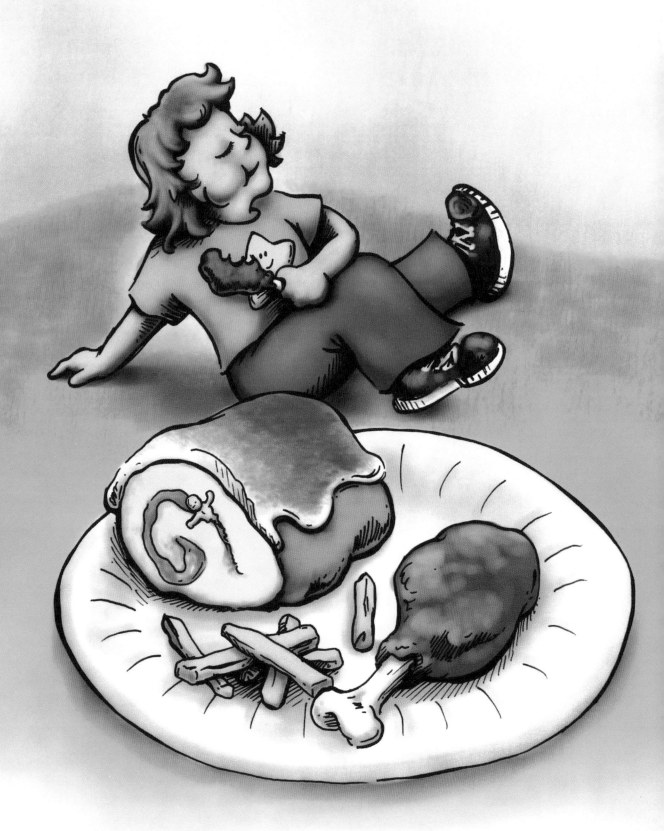

"I like

being in

my ladder

because

it makes

me

taller

than

everyone!"

"But, I don't like
when the day
is over!"

"Beads on trees!"
yelled Mom with
much surprise.

"Good eye, Mom!
Now you see
them, too!"
cheered
Ruby Rose.

Mom explained, "We can remember all of our favorite things about Mardi Gras any time we see...

"BEADS ON TREES!"
they chanted together.

BEADS ON TREES!

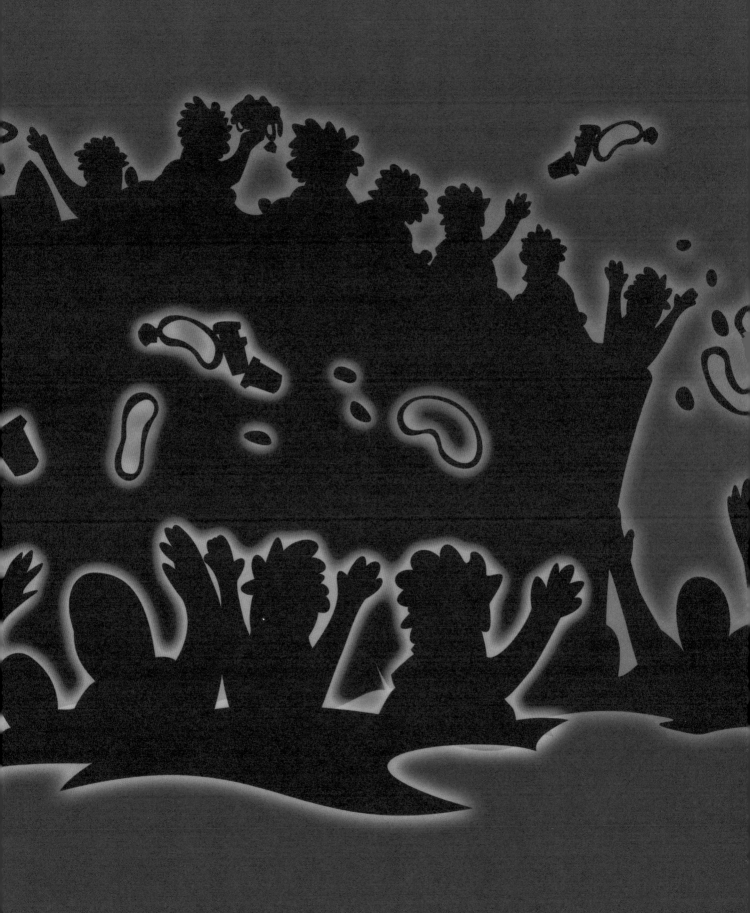